MELINDA

A Mostly Magnificent Moose

Story & Illustrations
by
Daniel Burch Fiddler

AuthorHouse™
1663 Liberty Drive, Suite 200
Bloomington, IN 47403
www.authorhouse.com
Phone: 1-800-839-8640

First published by AuthorHouse 4/10/2008

ISBN: 978-1-4343-8265-8 (sc)

Library of Congress Control Number: 2008903378

Printed in the United States of America
Bloomington, Indiana

This book is printed on acid-free paper.

Melinda had every reason
to be a mostly happy moose,
but she was not.

As you all know most moose are mostly magnificent and Melinda was no exception. She was the daughter of mostly magnificent moose parents. Melinda had a marvelous moose mother who took most excellent care of her. She had a most majestic moose father who took most excellent care of their family.

Melinda had every reason to be a mostly happy moose, but she was not.

Melinda lived in the wonderful, woodsiest, wilderness of western Wisconsin. There were lots of tantalizing, tender twigs to munch on. There were lots of wonderfully, watery water plants to eat. As you all know most moose mostly love to eat watery water plants and to munch on tantalizing, tender twigs.

Melinda had every reason to be a mostly happy moose, but she was not.

You see Melinda wanted something and she wanted it very badly.

"When will I get big awesome antlers just like daddy has?" Melinda would ask endlessly.

"Only boy moose get antlers," her mother would tell her, endlessly.

"But they are so beautiful. I want some," Melinda would say endlessly.

Finally, one day her father explained,

"Girl moose, like you and your mother, NEVER get antlers."

"But I want some," Melinda whimpered.
"Sorry," said her father.
"But I really want some," Melinda whined.
"Sorry," said her mother.
"Not fair. Just not fair," Melinda cried, running into the woods to sulk.

Even without antlers Melinda had every reason to be a mostly happy moose,
but she was not.

Melinda sat beneath a large birch tree deep in the woods sulking. She sulked and sulked. And then she sulked some more.

"It's just not fair that only boy moose have big awesome antlers," Melinda mumbled. "It's just not fair."

Most moose mostly know that sulking seldom solves serious problems and Melinda was no exception.

“Sitting here sulking and feeling sorry for myself will not get me antlers,” Melinda thought. “There must be a way to add the adornment of awesome antlers to my anatomy,” she added, as she arose and headed for home.

“Tomorrow morning I am going to find a way to get my very own antlers.”

The next morning Melinda left her parents who were eating wonderfully watery water plants and walked into the woods in search of a way to get her very own antlers.

As she walked deeper into the woods Melinda met Delilah, the delightful daughter of a darling deer family.

"Good morning Delilah."

"Good morning Melinda," Delilah answered. "Where are you going?"

"I'm going to find a way to get my very own antlers."

"Antlers?" Delilah asked. "Girls don't get antlers. My brother Darren the deer is definitely developing dashing antlers but we girls will never have them."

"Not fair. Just not fair," Melinda whined. "Antlers are so awesome and I want some."

"Sorry," said Delilah.

Even without antlers Melinda had every reason to be a mostly happy moose,
but she was not.

Melinda walked deeper into the woods. She soon came upon a clearing with a pond in the middle. There she noticed a tree with many branches covered with bright leaves.

She had an idea. Melinda bit off two branches and stuck one behind each ear.

She looked at her reflection in the pond.

"Wow! Now I have awesome antlers just like the majestic men moose have."

Melinda ran through the woods singing.
"I have awesome antlers."
"I have awesome antlers."

As she ran, Melinda ran into Delilah again.

“Look Delilah, I have awesome antlers,” Melinda said, dancing around and around.

“Those are not antlers,” Delilah said. “Those are branches covered with bright leaves and they make you look silly.”

Melinda knew Delilah was right. They were just branches covered with bright leaves, not real antlers. She removed them from behind her ears and began to cry.

"Not fair. Just not fair."

Even without leafy branch antlers Melinda had every reason to be a mostly happy moose,
but she was not.

Melinda walked back to the clearing with the pond. There she noticed the pond was surrounded by very large feathery fern plants.

She had an idea. Melinda bit off two large ferns and stuck one behind each ear.

She looked at her reflection in the pond.

"Wow! Now I have awesome antlers just like the majestic men moose have."

Melinda ran through the woods singing.
"I have awesome antlers."
"I have awesome antlers."

As she ran, Melinda ran into Delilah again.

"Look Delilah, I have awesome antlers," Melinda said, dancing around and around.

"Those are not antlers," Delilah said. "Those are feathery fern plants and they make you look silly."

Melinda knew Delilah was right. They were just feathery fern plants, not real antlers. She removed them from behind her ears and began to cry.

"Not fair. Just not fair."

Even without feathery fern antlers Melinda had every reason to be a mostly happy moose,
but she was not.

Melinda walked back to the clearing with the pond. There she noticed the clearing was filled with deliciously delightful daisies.

She had an idea. Melinda bit off two large daisies and stuck one behind each ear.

She looked at her reflection in the pond.

"Wow! Now I have awesome antlers just like the majestic men moose have."

Melinda ran through the woods singing.
"I have awesome antlers."
"I have awesome antlers."

As she ran, Melinda ran into Delilah again.

"Look Delilah, I have awesome antlers," Melinda said, dancing around and around.

"Those are not antlers," Delilah said. "Those are delightful daisies and they make you look like a mostly magnificent GIRL moose.

Melinda ran back to the clearing with the pond and looked at her reflection. She really was a mostly magnificent moose.

A mostly magnificent GIRL moose.

Melinda ran through the woods singing.
“Who needs antlers?”
“Who needs antlers?”

With daisies instead of antlers Melinda had every reason to be a mostly happy moose.

And she was.

To Joan and all the Idyllwild writers for their help
For the twins Aidan and Casey

LaVergne, TN USA
15 January 2010
170102LV00001B

9781434382658